For Gray, Trey, Logan,
Heidi, Finley, Suzanna, Oliver,
and the little ones yet to join the family.
May your imaginations always soar!

With Love,
Bama

Children's
Picture Book

www.mascotbooks.com

Pete the Hungry Pig

©2019 Sue Wambolt. All Rights Reserved. No part of this publication may be reproduced, stored in a retrieval system or transmitted in any form by any means electronic, mechanical, or photocopying, recording or otherwise without the permission of the author.

For more information, please contact:
Mascot Books
620 Herndon Parkway, Suite 320
Herndon, VA 20170
info@mascotbooks.com

Library of Congress Control Number: 2019909388

CPSIA Code: PRT0819A
ISBN-13: 978-1-64307-515-0

Printed in the United States

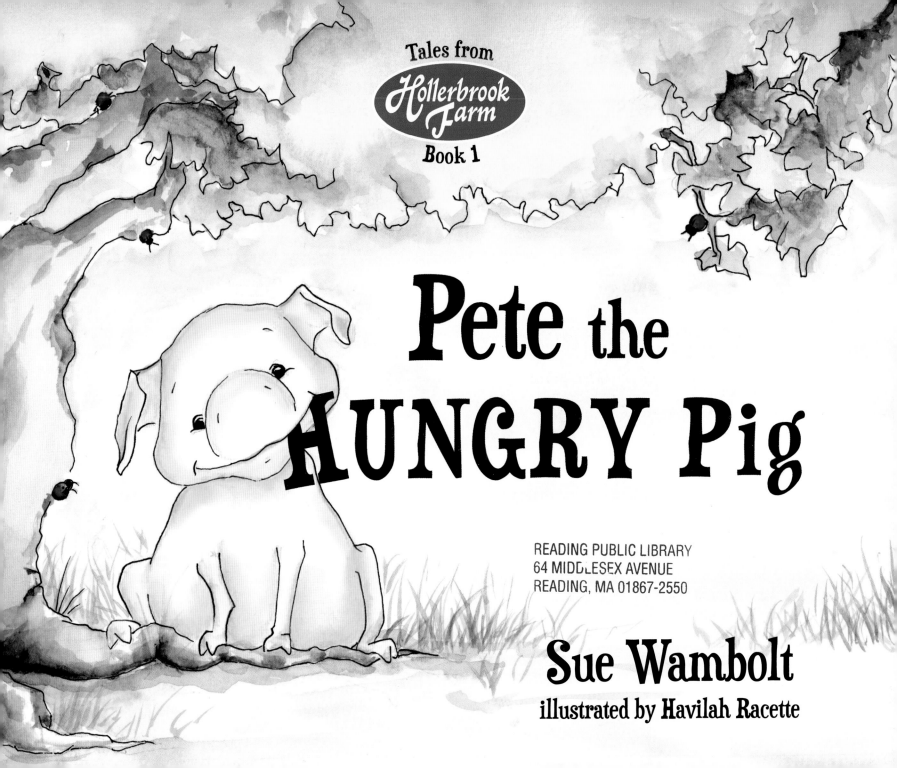

Tales from
Hollerbrook Farm
Book 1

Pete the HUNGRY Pig

Sue Wambolt

illustrated by Havilah Racette

In the east of Kentucky in the town of Ash River
was a small country farm run by old Owen McShiver.
Hollerbrook Farm, it was named years ago,
had an entrance of apple trees lined in a row.

At the end of the long, twisty dirt road you'd find
a little white house on a hill, just the kind
with a long farmers porch and an old wooden swing.
It was a place Owen thought that was fit for a king.

Owen sat on his swing and admired his farm—
the long rolling meadows and quaint country charm.
There were orchards of blueberries and gardens galore,
and a sea of wildflowers right by the back door.

Owen smiled as he watched the animals at play,
sitting on the porch, just swinging away.
With thirty acres of fields and a sprawling oak tree,
the farm was a beauty—I'm sure you'd agree.

On the farm Owen ran with his wife named Flo
were a horse named Breeze and a cow named Joe.
There was Ned the sheep and his brother, Jed,
a goat named Rose, and her husband, Fred.

There was a new piglet in the barn, just two days old,
a little boy named Pete, or so we were told.
He had a curly little tail and a wrinkled snout.
He fit right in—without a doubt!

Of course there was a dog—an old basset hound—
who wandered around and around and around.
The dog's name was Scotty. He was gentle and sweet,
and could often be found with his pig friend, Pete.
He was brown all over with a white spot on his nose,
and often tripped on his ears that hung way past his toes!

This was the scene at the farm each day.
It was pretty much perfect in every way.
The sun came up at half past five,
the animals started stirring—
the farm came alive!
The rooster started crowing from
a-top the barn door.
Owen jumped out of bed—
his feet hit the floor!

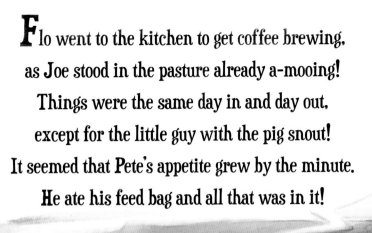

Flo went to the kitchen to get coffee brewing,
as Joe stood in the pasture already a-mooing!
Things were the same day in and day out,
except for the little guy with the pig snout!
It seemed that Pete's appetite grew by the minute.
He ate his feed bag and all that was in it!

I guess the word "little" no longer applied
to Pete who ate everything—or at least he tried!
There were stripes in the garden from one end to the other
as Pete plowed through the plants, one after another.
He ate the eggs from right under the chickens.
He ate and he ate, the little dickens!

HEIDI'S HEN HOUSE CO.

Pete ate the fence around his pen,
took a snooze in the sun, then started again!
He ate the saddle off Breeze the horse,
and got a stomach ache, of course!
But that did not stop him, the hungry pig.
He ate the barn door—and it sure was big!

Instead of swinging on the porch each day,
watching his animals out at play,
Owen was busy with his hammer and nails
repairing the tractors, the fences, and pails.

Pete's mischief had caused quite a stir on the farm,
causing fear and anger and even alarm
to those poor little animals, the chicks and the hens,
who ran when they saw him to the rear of their pens.

Nothing was safe on Hollerbrook Farm anymore—
not the gates or the gardens or the big barn door.
There were even bites taken out of the old oak tree,
which seems rather silly, wouldn't you agree?

When Pete walked down the driveway he left a trail,
including parts of the mailbox and some of the mail.
One day there were pieces of the wheel from the plow.
He ate it, I know, but I'm just not sure how.

Hollerbrook Farm
Heidi Girl Way
Ash River, KY

From Mom

Poor Owen McShiver did not know what to do;
the farm was a mess and he was, too.
Pete could not stay if he kept on eating,
Owen said it before, but it bears repeating.

The word was out about the farm's hungry pig—
can you guess who showed up doing a jig?
It was Butch the butcher who came a-knockin'
while Owen sat quietly on his porch a-rockin'.

Butch whistled a tune as he walked to the door
and offered old Owen so very much more
than he could have imagined for his hungry pig Pete,
that Owen fell from his swing and jumped to his feet!

"I can take him right now," Butch said with a grin.
"I'll bring my truck over and pop him right in."
Old Owen was tempted to accept Butch's price
but Flo interrupted with a word of advice.

"**R**emember," she said, "the sign that we read
on the back of the truck of farmer Ted?
The County Fair, it seems, is at the town square
but I fear, my dear, we have no time to spare.
The pig-judging contest is today at two,
so this is what I propose we do. . ."

"...give Pete a bath and get rid of the flies
and give him a shot at winning first prize.
The prize money would cover the repairs on the farm
and save poor Pete from the butcher's harm.

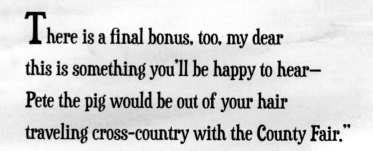

There is a final bonus, too, my dear
this is something you'll be happy to hear—
Pete the pig would be out of your hair
traveling cross-country with the County Fair."

When Flo looked at Owen, he had a big smile.
Then he thought about it for a while.
He bid the butcher a fond farewell,
shook his hand, and started to yell!
This was the best news he had heard all day
for he knew in his heart that Pete couldn't stay.

It was already noon and there was no time to spare;
they needed to get Pete to the County Fair.
They rounded him up and brought him out back
and dusted him off with an empty feed sack.
They scrubbed ole Pete from his head to his toes,
then rinsed him all over with the garden hose.

They greased him up from bottom to top,
then polished him quickly with the kitchen mop!
Pete sure looked great—he was squeaky clean.
He was the best-looking pig they had ever seen!
In no time at all he was in Owen's truck
as Flo waved from the porch and bid them good luck.

Owen arrived at the fair with Pete by his side.
He was so happy, he could have cried.
Crowds began to gather and fill the tent
as Pete arrived for the big event.
The judges looked the pigs over and took some notes,
then gathered together and added up votes.

WEAZE   TOOZLE   PETE   ZANNA   OLLIE

The loudspeaker echoed across the fairground
to the countryfolk who had gathered around.
It was loud and it was clear
so all the fair goers were sure to hear:

THE BLUE RIBBON PIG AT THE COUNTY FAIR
IS A PIG WHO EATS FAR MORE THAN HIS SHARE.
HE'S BIG AND ROUND AND FULL OF CHARM—
HE'S PETE THE PIG FROM HOLLERBROOK FARM!

Pete won the blue ribbon; he came in first place
and managed to save old **O**wen's place.
The cash award would pay the repairs—
just don't tell **O**wen about the stairs!

With a whistle and a puff, he was off and away
after what could be called a pretty wonderful day.
He was glowing—if that's possible—from his head to his feet
as his stomach started to grumble for something to eat!

And as Pete headed out in the County Fair train,
there were some things he had to explain.
I don't have to tell you what he was doing,
but I'll give you a hint. . .he was chewing!

*C*lickety-clack, clickety-clack,
Pete munched on the train as it rolled down the track.
Clickety-clack, clickety-clack,
He was off on an adventure and never looked back.